Red-Dirt Jessie

Red-Dirt Jessie

Anna Myers

Walker and Company New York

For my husband, Paul,
who is my partner in everything.

All the characters and events portrayed in this work are fictitious.

First published in the United States of America in hardcover in 1992 by Walker Publishing Company, Inc.; first paperback edition published in 1994.

Published simultaneously in Canada by Thomas Allen & Son Canada, Limited, Markham, Ontario

The Library of Congress cataloged the hardcover edition of this book as follows:
Myers, Anna.
Red-dirt Jessie / Anna Myers.
p. cm.
Summary: Jessie, a young girl living in the Oklahoma dust bowl during the Depression, tries to tame a wild dog and help her father recover from a nervous breakdown.
ISBN 0-8027-8172-1
[1. Fathers—Fiction. 2. Dogs—Fiction.
3. Depressions—1929—Fiction.
4. Oklahoma—Fiction.] I. Title.
PZ7.M9814Re 1992
[Fic]—dc20 92-244
CIP
AC

ISBN 0-8027-7435-0

Printed in the United States of America

2 4 6 8 10 9 7 5 3 1

·O·N·E·

❁

My little sister Patsy is dead. Papa made the box from part of the tumbled-down chicken house. He stood out there in the scorching July sun and worked on that box, just smoothing and smoothing on that old wood. There was a great big oak tree right near, but Papa stayed in the sun.

Up under the catalpa tree Uncle Delbert was digging the grave. My little brother, H.J., which is short for Hobert Joseph after Papa, played with his little tin car in the red dirt that piled up around the edge of the hole. I thought maybe it wasn't right, him playing in the dirt from a grave, but I didn't call to him or go up there to scold. H.J. was used to playing with Patsy, and now he couldn't. Not ever again.

Mama and Aunt Maybell got Patsy ready in the kitchen, her on a blanket on the table. Aunt Maybell put the blue gingham dress on her little body. It was too small to button in the back, but it looked nice from the front. Mama sent me to get Patsy's doll, Mary Beth.

I found it on the top of the chiffonier that belonged to Grandma years ago. Back in the kitchen Mama took the doll and started to put it beside Patsy, but she didn't. My mama just stood there cradling Mary Beth like Patsy always did and rocking back and forth. I couldn't stand to watch, so I bolted out the kitchen door.

I went out to Papa. He had stopped working and was just standing there wiping sweat from his face with his big red bandanna. Then he looked at me and held out his arms. Leaning against his big chest, I started to cry. Papa didn't cry, but his heart was broke. Under his blue chambray shirt and hairy skin his heart was just in pieces. I could tell by the way he held me.

I wished there was something to say, some way to make him feel better. My mind kept grabbing at words. I considered talking about the oatmeal. "You got it for her," I could have said, but I wasn't sure it would be a thing Papa wanted to remember.

"Eat something, sweetie," Mama told Patsy that morning.

It was me that mentioned the oatmeal, something she would eat even when the fever bothered her.

"You know we don't have no oatmeal, Jessie. And there ain't no way to get any." Mama turned back to take the biscuits out of the oven.

It was true. "I can't give you no more credit," Mr. Hensen had told Papa two weeks earlier with me standing there beside him, all red-faced.

"Come on, sugar." Mama had put her hand on Patsy's forehead. "We got some syrup to put on the biscuits."

Papa got up from the table, leaving his egg untouched. He didn't say nothing, just walked out the door without a word.

"H.J.," said Mama in a sort of flat voice. "Here, eat your papa's egg."

We didn't see Papa again until evening. When the screen door slammed, we ran in to see him setting a box of Quaker Oats on the table. Mama was staring at him.

"Maud," he said, and his voice had cracks in it. "A man's got to do something. Some little thing."

I wondered if he stole to bring home that round box of oats. Of course Mama was wondering too, but we didn't say nothing, even to each other. I went back to washing the bean pot, but that's when the terrible truth came to me. I knew for sure how sick Patsy was, and I knew for sure that Papa and Mama both believed Patsy was going to die.

And she did. Laid back in the middle of a cough and closed her eyes. "Just tuckered out," said Papa. "Just tuckered out from fighting that damn pneumonia."

I felt awful sad about losing my little sister, and I felt so scared of the look on Papa's face, like maybe he was dying too.

When Patsy first got sick, old Doc Johnson came out to see her. Papa tried to give him some money, but Doc said he'd rather have eggs, which we knew wasn't true but was good of him to say. "Might be the electuary will help," Doc said to Mama and Papa about the medicine he had left.

They were out on the porch, with me around by the edge behind the big red hollyhocks, sort of hunched down and listening.

"Keep her cool and away from the others." A stream of Doc's tobacco shot through the air and landed at my feet. "Else you might have a house full of feverish young ones."

"We'll do that," Papa said. "But the older

ones—Jessie and H.J. They're right strong, not likely to come down sick."

"Like the blackjack trees." Mama's voice was soft, and I had to strain to hear. "Not requiring much, not getting much, but they just keep growing."

"And you, ma'am," said the doctor. "I hope you're strong, because you're going to need a heap of strength."

Mama had it. All through Patsy's sickness she just prayed and worked. And when her baby died there was a new bend in her shoulders, but she was still strong.

It was Papa who couldn't stand it. It was Papa who would get up from rocking Patsy and go outside. He'd take a hoe and chop at the weeds in the garden or an ax and go at a log that didn't need splitting till winter. Most times he'd not even hear the call to supper. Mama would go out and touch him on the shoulder, take his hand, and sort of lead him back to the house. It was Papa that was near about to break. Me and Mama both knew, but we didn't say nothing, even to each other, because neither one of us knew what words to use about Papa going to pieces.

Neighbors came to watch us bury Patsy in that

big red hole under the catalpas. The sun was awful hot. I put my hand up to shade my eyes. We sang "Amazing Grace," and the preacher said some things. After he was finished Aunt Maybell came up and hugged me. I thought I ought to hug her back, but I didn't. I just stood there, and it was like my insides were made from part of that chicken house wall.

The days after Patsy died stretched out before us like a long, dusty road of summer. "Ain't you going to gather the corn?" Mama asked Papa.

"Can't get but eight cents a bushel. Not hardly worth it." Papa didn't even get up from his chair.

"Might get enough to buy flour and beans." Mama walked away from the stove, where we were working at canning tomatoes, and went to the window to look out at the cornfield. "'Coons'll get it sure if we don't pretty soon."

"I'll get it directly," said Papa, but he didn't move.

Later Mama, H.J., and me went down to the field, and we pulled about ten bushels to sell. "Uncle Delbert can take this to town for us come

Saturday," said Mama. "We'll save the rest for eating and feed."

When we got back to the kitchen, Papa was still there, alone in the evening shadows. I thought Mama would tell him about the corn, but she didn't. "I'll make some gravy," she said, sort of hardy and cheerful. Papa didn't eat more than two bites. I didn't either, even though down in the corn patch hunger had been gnawing at me. There across the round table from Papa I couldn't swallow gravy or biscuits, because in the lamplight I could see that there just wasn't no life in my Papa's gray eyes.

Mama was too tired to stir when she was done eating, so I gathered up the plates and carried them over to the wash pan. At Papa's place I reached for his dish, but instead I put out my hand and rested it on his big one. I used to love to have his huge fingers wrapped around mine, but his hand didn't even feel right, and he didn't glance up at me. Papa's hands and Papa's eyes were cold. A shiver went over me right there in July in our hot kitchen.

Days were awful hard with Papa just rocking away the hours in Grandma's old cane-bottom rocker or sometimes standing out on the porch leaning against a rail and staring out over the land like he was watching for something that never came. Mama and me sort of worked around him, canning what we could from our garden. Sometimes I'd do things like take him a glass of water. I would rest my hand on his shoulder and try to interest him in the new baby chickens or the calf. He might say something like "That's fine," but there wasn't no meaning to his words. And there wasn't no reflection of me in his eyes. It was like maybe he didn't really see me, like I wasn't important at all.

"Give him a little time," Mama said. "Your papa is hurt way down deep, but he will mend. Time eases heartache some."

Bedtime was even worse than the daylight hours. I had always been sort of uneasy if I woke up in the night. Nothing ever sounded friendly to me after dark. The cry of a hoot owl floating through the shadowy trees could make me feel so lonesome, and the howl of coyotes from some dark hill gave me goose bumps all over my arms. Even before Patsy died, our whole place seemed different to me when it was late and quiet. After grief spread through every board of the house and seeped out to the red earth, I dreaded Mama's good-night kiss, because it signaled that the day was over.

One terrible night something woke me in the middle of a dream. It was a sound carried by the soft summer breeze through my south window. I got up and crept over to the sill to look out. The moon was big and round in the sky, lighting up the side of our old red barn and the hill in the front pasture. The noise came again, and for a minute I thought it was Bossy bawling for her calf, but then I saw the form. Papa walking off over the rise, almost out of sight. Papa crying out to the night like some hurt animal. It was my papa walking and crying in the dark. I pushed the window down hard, ran back to bed, and buried my face and ears deep in the feather pillow.

After a while I moved the pillow and waited for Papa's step on the porch or the closing of the screen door, but the only thing I heard was the ticking of Grandma's clock from the front room. He didn't come back. Sometime before dawn I went back to sleep, wishing it was me buried up under the catalpa, because then I would never have had to hear the terribleness of Papa's misery in the night.

·T·W·O·

Nothing on our place seemed to have much life those July days except H.J. "Little ones play, no matter what," said Mama, and I knew that his games were a comfort to her.

One morning he stayed a long time digging a hole out by the garden. When I called at noon, I watched him run to the house dragging the big shovel after him. "I got to hurry," he said at the table, as he pushed spoons of beans real quick into his mouth.

"Why?" asked Mama, handing him some corn bread.

"I'm fixing to hit China by tomorrow sure."

Me and Mama looked at each other, not wanting to disappoint him with the truth. I remembered how the summer before H.J. and Patsy had spent lots of time collecting locust shells.

"Hey," I said. "Why don't you hold off on China till you're bigger, in case them China people don't like you busting in on their dinner or something." I stopped to stir some pepper sauce into my beans. "I was just thinking how I'd give my quarter for some locust shells. Fifty, though. I'd need me fifty." I took a bite and then cautioned, "Wholes. I don't want no pieces."

I ran to get the coin. Aunt Maybell had given me the money for helping her plant potatoes in the spring on a day I liked to remember. We were in a hurry on account of it being the day the *Farmer's Almanac* said was right for planting and us getting a late start. We worked real fast without talking much until Aunt Maybell said, "Lands, we got to rest a minute."

It was hot, and she took off her straw hat to fan herself. Sprawled beside her, I stuck my hand down in the earth Uncle Delbert had turned up with the plow. "Papa says the ground ain't red everywhere," I commented.

"That's so. Not even all over this state." Aunt Maybell held up a handful of dirt and let it sift out of her hand in a red stream. "But it is sure enough red here. Stubborn, too. Won't come out of nothing on wash day."

I gathered a fistful and made my own red stream. "I like it red," I announced.

Aunt Maybell shook her head in agreement. "I

figure it makes us strong, seeps under our skin and makes us too blamed stubborn to give up when things turn rough."

It was just last spring, but after all our trouble it seemed so long ago that I was excited about getting a quarter. I had kept the coin wrapped in a handkerchief pushed to the back of a drawer in Grandma's chiffonier. But now money didn't interest me much. I took it out and held it up to show H.J., turning it to catch the sunlight. "It would buy licorice sticks," I told him. "And peppermints, and even a bottle of soda pop."

He was interested. Then his face screwed up with doubt. "We don't hardly get to town no more. Papa ain't even trying to fix the truck at all."

"Well," I said, "probably we could go with Uncle Delbert some Saturday." I stopped and gave him a long look. "Of course, you might not be able to find fifty."

"I can do it all right," he said, and he smiled the first real smile I'd seen around our place for a long time.

It made me feel good to see H.J. fired up about something. I told him about how the locust left its thin shell when it was full growed and about how the singing was on account of looking for a mate. That was the kind of stuff Papa used to tell us, but now Papa wasn't talking about insects or nothing else.

One scorching afternoon H.J. took his locust shells from the big cigar box and spread them in a line across the porch so that I could help him count them. I'd say the numbers, with him repeating each one after me.

"How many more?" he asked when we finished with twenty-nine. I wasn't real good at figuring in my head, so I scratched the problem in the porch dust. "Just twenty-one more."

"Hot dog!" He leaned over to study my arithmetic. "I aim to learn how to do that on the first day of school." He traced the figures with his dirty little finger.

"Maybe not the very first day," I cautioned him, "but you'll learn all right. Truth is, I've learned as much about numbers as I hanker after knowing, but I'm not through, I reckon. Anyway, school's awful fun, 'specially the reading part, and come fall you will be walking down that road right beside me." I pointed north toward our schoolhouse two miles away.

"I'm pretty big now." He stood up, and he smiled. Every time H.J. smiled I thought how I'd give lots and lots of quarters if I had them just to see that grin.

It was the only hopeful thing there was to look at, my little brother standing on the porch steps as straight as he could, his overalls too short for his growing legs. "High-water pants" Papa would have called them, except that Papa didn't look at H.J. much anymore.

For myself there wasn't anything to care about. Mama's promise about Papa starting to heal didn't appear likely to come true. I sat there fingering the locusts' shells and listening to their singing in the trees, thinking how I'd never noticed before that it was awful sad. The July heat seemed to rise up and mix somehow with the hurt hanging around our whole sixty acres and then come out in the sound of the locusts, way too mournful for courting music.

It was that very afternoon that Aunt Maybell came panting to our door. Mama had just come up from the garden with her apron full of okra. I followed her into the kitchen. H.J. was still on the porch and called out, "Yonder comes Aunt Maybell."

Papa didn't even look toward the window, but me and Mama went right out. From the way she moved, quick and determined like, we could see that Aunt Maybell had a purpose for her visit. Of course, she wouldn't have walked the mile from her place on such a hot day without reason.

Maybe it'll be good news, I said to myself, straining to see our visitor's face. I was afraid to say it out loud because it ain't lucky to do such.

"Run get some water from the bucket," Mama told me. "She'll be needing a bit of cool."

In the kitchen I couldn't resist trying. "Aunt Maybell looks like she's got something on her mind, moving right along." I glanced over at Papa as I splashed up a dipper of water, but he just kept rocking. I went back on out.

"Lands I'm tuckered." Aunt Maybell reached for the water and dropped her big body into the porch chair. Me, Mama, and H.J. stood there, waiting and watching as she drank real slow, then threw the last bit on the hollyhocks. Even though the drought was over, not one of us ever wasted even a drop of water.

Mama raised her eyebrow and cocked one eye.

"You going to tell us why you come over here practically running?"

"Well," said Aunt Maybell, enjoying the suspense, "it's quite a story."

"Tell," demanded H.J. I didn't say anything because I liked the waiting. It had been so long since anything interesting had come along to wait for.

"Delbert's working on the truck." Aunt Maybell leaned back in her chair with a smile.

"So," said Mama. "What's new about that? Delbert's always working on the truck."

"Not like this time! Delbert's working on the truck because we're fixing to head for California!" She reached out quickly for Mama's hand. "Come with us, Maud. You just got to come with us."

I sucked in my breath real quick with surprise, and my eyes shot to Mama's face.

"California?" Mama was shaking her head. "What the devil are you talking about?"

"Work." Aunt Maybell stood up. "Delbert's brother wrote about how there is work aplenty picking up fruit and all." She rolled her eyes at me and H.J. "Even the young ones could work."

"I'll work," I said. "I'll work so hard."

"Me too." H.J. was jumping up and down.

"Hold your horses." Mama shot us a warning look, then turned back to Aunt Maybell. "Delbert's brother. How long is it he's been out there now?"

"Three months. Worked every day. Says the weather is just something to behold."

I remembered hearing about Uncle Delbert's brother and his family, how their land in the western part of the state just blew away bit by bit in great dust storms until there wasn't a thing left. Papa said we were awful lucky not to live out there in the middle of blowing dirt, but that was before Patsy got sick. I stood there thinking that maybe if we had lived in the dust and picked up and left we might have got away before death and heartbreak found us.

"Well?" Aunt Maybell had her hand on Mama's arm again. "I'd worry did we go off and leave you here. Hobert like he is."

"I don't know." Mama's face was twisted with doubt. "I don't know as he'd go." She motioned toward the house. "Or if it'd be right."

"It's time," said Aunt Maybell, "that I talked to that brother of mine." With a determined whirl, she turned and marched into the house. Mama followed. Me and H.J. made movements too, but Mama put out her hand to signal stop and shook her head.

As soon as Mama's back disappeared into the house, I ran around the corner to the open kitchen window. H.J. was right behind me. As I hunkered down with my head just below the sill, I put my fingers to my lips in a hush message for H.J.

Aunt Maybell was talking. "Hobert," she said, her voice strong enough to carry easily to where I waited in a tight listening ball, "you got two other young ones to consider. And Maud. Think what you're handing to her."

It was quiet for a bit. Maybe Papa was talking, but if he was I couldn't hear him. More likely he was just rocking.

"You got two left, Hobert." I could hear Aunt Maybell crying now. "That's more than some of us was ever blessed with." I remembered how Mama had told me that Aunt Maybell never did have any babies and that she had wanted to have some real bad.

Again it was quiet. Then Aunt Maybell's voice boomed out, yelling and angry. "One of these days, Brother, you will be called on to get up from that chair. Else you might lose the two kids God let you keep!" I could hear her stomping out of the room, and then the door slammed.

H.J. pulled on my dress tail. "Are we going to California?" he asked. "Are we?"

I shook my head. "No, I reckon we ain't going nowhere." I kicked real hard at what I thought was a clod of dirt, but when my bare toe touched it, I realized I'd kicked a toad. H.J. ran over to pick it up, but it hopped off. Toads are pretty sturdy. I wasn't. "I didn't mean to hurt nothing," I said, and started to cry.

"Don't cry about the toad." H.J. came over and put his small hand on my shoulder. "I done something bad once too."

I could tell he wanted to get something off his chest. "What?" I asked, and I wiped my eyes on the back of my fist.

"You know that old yeller cat that used to hang around the barn some?" H.J.'s voice was low and full of importance. "Well, one day I wet on that cat. Right on his back. On purpose, just to see if he'd run."

I almost laughed, and it gave me energy to get up and move. "We ain't perfect, I reckon," I said to H.J.

When Aunt Maybell left, she said they'd come

by on their way the next day in case we had decided to go.

"Come around to say good-bye," Mama told her, "but I reckon we'll just stay here. We got the chickens and the eggs and Bossy and her calf. We got the land. Hobert sets lots of store in the land."

"Hobert's sick," said Aunt Maybell. "I'm stopping in town tomorrow to send out Doc. I don't know as I ought to go off with my brother like he is." She tried to make her worried face into a smile. "Delbert, though, he's right determined to see California. Maybe we won't stay long, and could be Hobert will be all better when we get back, and prices up to make growing worth it again." She reached out and patted my hair.

She was back the next morning, driving up with Uncle Delbert in their old truck and blowing the horn just as Mama was taking the breakfast biscuits out of the oven. Generally she wouldn't let bread get cold for nothing, but Mama left it on the table and ran with me and H.J. out the front door.

"We got to hurry," Uncle Delbert said as Aunt Maybell crawled out. "Want to make Texas by dark."

"You could still come, Maud." Aunt Maybell

pointed to the back of the truck, piled high with a mattress on top. "Plenty of room for riding."

Mama shook her head. "Well, then we got to go." She turned to me. "Jessie, you and H.J. go over to our place once in a while and get what's left in the garden. We got two hens. Coyotes will get them sure if you don't take a gunnysack over there and tote them here." She reached out and put her arm around me. "There's Ring too. I feel plum miserable about leaving that dog, even if he has took to wandering with the coyotes. Should you see him, give him a kind word and a crust of bread. His mama was a sure fine animal, but he's always been sort of on the wild side. Never quite belonged to us." She looked back to the truck, where Uncle Delbert waited.

"Come in and say good-bye to Hobert," urged Mama. "You'll not feel right do you not."

This time no one stopped us, so H.J. and me followed them in.

"I'm going now, Hobert." Aunt Maybell talked real loud, like Papa was deaf and she was trying to make him hear her.

Papa turned and looked at her, but he didn't say nothing. "Mark my words," she said. "You have to get out of that chair one of these days and take a hold again." Aunt Maybell was crying, and this time she didn't stomp out of the room, just walked real soft with her head down.

I hurried up to be beside her. "I wanted to touch him," she said to me, "but it ain't ever been our way."

I put my arm around her big waist. "Papa will be all right," I said. "And I'll take care of Ring. Papa and Ring will both be OK when you come back."

"Bless you, child," she said. "If work's good in California, I'm going to send you a little something."

Then she climbed up into the truck, and Uncle Delbert started the motor. We all waved as they drove off. Mama had great big tears running down her face. I knew she was thinking that there wasn't anyone now to help us. With Aunt Maybell and Uncle Delbert gone, there wasn't no one to help fight off the big money problems people called the Depression or to help us pull Papa back to the land of the living.

We stood there waving and watching till there wasn't no more sight of the old truck. Then we went back inside to eat breakfast. Mama didn't notice me much, so I took three biscuits that I didn't aim to eat. Instead, when she wasn't looking, I wrapped them in a piece of old dish towel. I was laying a plan concerning Aunt Maybell's dog, Ring.

Come the cool of the evening, when it was about time for chickens to roost, I'd take two gunnysacks and H.J. We'd go over to fetch back the hens. Maybe we'd see Ring. Maybe I would call to him and hold out a biscuit. Maybe he'd follow us home. We hadn't had a dog since Old Scraps died last winter. A dog would be a friend to walk with, and for H.J. to run with. Papa liked dogs too. Ring was pretty young. Might be Papa would take an interest and train him for rabbit hunting like Old Scraps used to. It would be awful good for Papa, going out to hunt and bringing home meat for Mama to fry up.

"Here, Ring," I said real softly, lost in my own thoughts. "Here, boy."

"What'd you say?" Mama asked.

"Nothing," I said. "Nothing, Mama." I went on picking up the breakfast dishes. I decided not to ask about bringing Ring home with us. Mama might fuss about having nothing to feed him. If Aunt Maybell had just come right out and told me to fetch him, Mama would have said it was all right. As it was, I'd have to show Mama what a nice dog he could be.

In the afternoon Mama sent me to pick okra. Usually I hated touching the sticky green pods, but the thought of Ring filled my mind, and I didn't even stop often to wipe my hands on the wet cloth carried in my pocket. I knew I was making too much of the dog, but I needed something to think about, something to work toward. Ring would be for me what the locust shells were for H.J. I skipped back from the garden with a half bucket of okra and volunteered to cut it up.

After supper I announced that I was taking H.J. and going over to Aunt Maybell's to get her hens.

Mama poured the heated water over the full dishpan. "We'll just let these set. We'll need to hurry if we want to get home before dark."

It wasn't how I'd planned it at all. "Mama," I said. "You're too tired to walk over there and back. Me and H.J. can do it our own selves just fine."

"H.J. can't carry no hen all the way back here." She looked at me. "I ain't so sure you're strong enough for that. Maybell's hens are Rhode Island reds. They're right big creatures."

I was disappointed, but I knew Mama was right. Anyway, the trip home through the shadows wouldn't be so scary with her along.

It felt good, walking along with the sun about

to set and looking forward to something. H.J. didn't even know about my plan, but he was excited too. Even Mama seemed to have a little more spirit in her face and in how she moved, like maybe it helped to get away from our place, where Patsy's grave sort of filled all sixty acres and where Papa was just about as dead as Patsy.

I wanted to sing something like "Red River Valley," but I thought Mama might not like me singing because Patsy always liked for me to sing to her. It was real funny how just when I was thinking that, H.J. started to hum that very tune. Mama gave him a little smile, and I felt good all over.

"Things are going to get better. I can promise you two young ones that. Things seem sort of black right now, but they will get better." Mama's voice sounded sure, and she held her head up straight and certain.

It was just then that I saw Ring. He was standing on a little hill of red sandrock, and he was watching us as we got close to Aunt Maybell's house. I didn't call to him, but I looked at him, and I sent him a message right from my heart.

·T·H·R·E·E·

❁

Aunt Maybell's house seemed real lonely looking, like the front porch was missing Uncle Delbert being there messing with his fishing tackle. It was all closed up and empty, and I felt sad seeing the lonesome chimney with no fire coming from the kitchen stove.

We turned away from the empty house and went straight to the garden. "There's a few green beans," Mama said. "We'll gather what's here." She gave us a brave little smile. "Your papa is real partial to fresh green beans."

Papa had practically quit eating. I doubted if green beans would make any difference, but I knew Mama would keep trying, because my mama just didn't give up. It was like Aunt Maybell said. Mama had the red dirt inside her, and it made her stubborn strong. I looked down at my hands and arms, wondering if the strength was inside me.

We picked squash too. I never did like green or

yellow squash, but I didn't say anything. Mama wouldn't put up with no talk about not wanting any certain food. "People standing in line to beg for a bowl of soup and you turning up your nose at good plain food like you're Lady Astor," she always told me.

I always meant to ask who Lady Astor was, but I never thought of it unless Mama mentioned her name. It wasn't a good time then to ask questions, because Mama was put out with me for being picky.

H.J. put the garden stuff in his gunnysack. "I could carry a hen and this junk too." He threw the sack over his shoulder. "It ain't heavy at all."

"Well," said Mama, giving the garden rows one last going over with her eyes. "There don't appear to be anything left here. We might as well head for the henhouse."

I stood still too, looking around for something that could be used as an excuse to slow us down. If we got the chickens and left now, there would be no chance to see Ring again. Maybe something would come up. A reason for delay would buy the time. Time for the tame part of Ring to remind him that he liked to hear a human voice call his name.

But there was nothing to stop us, and Mama was headed toward the chicken house. "H.J.," she said. "Once me and Jessie are inside, you close the door and lean there, so a hen flopping can't push it open."

We walked around the side of the barn. Mama was in front, then me and H.J., but she didn't notice Ring off to the side. "Mama." I spoke real soft, not wanting to scare him. I reached out and touched her arm. "Look." I held out my hand to the dog. "Here, Ring. Here."

He was a big, long-haired dog, solid black except for the white circle around his tail. I took a step toward him, and he turned, ready to run. "Be careful," Mama said. "He don't know you."

"Can we take him home?" H.J. yelled, and he bounded toward the dog.

Ring was gone in a flash. My heart was as droopy as the wilted tomato vine in Aunt Maybell's garden. The only good thing was watching that dog move, a quick, black streak against the pink and yellow sunset.

"Let's get them chickens," Mama said. H.J. started to say something, but I hushed him with my finger to my lips. Later we could ask again about the dog.

The hens didn't put up much of a fight. Mama reached out real quick and grabbed one right off the roost. The other one took to squawking and flapping her wings. I held the sack with the hen in it, and Mama chased the protesting one into a corner and snatched it up.

H.J. took his job as door guard right serious. "Move," Mama had to yell to him. "We got them now. Let us out."

"No," said H.J. "Not till you say we can have Ring for our dog. I ain't moving unless you promise."

I was horrified. Mama, I thought, will get him now, and there won't be any chance of us getting our way about that dog, not ever.

But then Mama did something real strange. She laughed. My Mama stood there in that smelly chicken house with a complaining hen sacked up and thrown over her shoulder, and she laughed. It sounded so odd, because I hadn't heard her make such a noise in a very long time. "Move, Mr. Big Britches," she demanded. "You move and we'll see."

"Well?" said my little brother as soon as we stepped out.

Mama tried to sound mad, but she wasn't. "If

that dog is fool enough to want to live at our place, I'll not stop him." She shifted the gunnysack to the other shoulder, and I could see a little smile sort of playing around her lips.

He's making things better already, I thought. Ring's done started to make things better.

Mama was right about the hen being real heavy. We had to stop a couple of times to rest on the way home, but I didn't mind the load or the ache in my arms and shoulders. Hope made me feel so strong.

In bed that night I didn't dread the sounds of darkness so much. I thought about how Ring might be out there. How he might have followed us home without us even knowing it. He might be out there looking at our house right now and remembering how I'd called his name.

In the morning I got up looking forward to the day. As soon as we'd done our chores, I planned, me and H.J. would head over to Aunt Maybell's. The biscuits I'd saved from yesterday were pretty hard, but I could find something to offer him. Might be he wouldn't follow us home today, but if we went every day, it would work. Papa always said creatures can tell how people feel, if they're afraid or not. Well, then, Ring would know. He would know that I loved him and that we needed a dog. We needed him real bad.

I was at the pump getting water to heat up for breakfast dishes when I saw the car coming. It was a familiar black Ford, but at first I couldn't think where I'd seen it before. Our neighbors all drove trucks, and this was a shiny car. When it stopped, I recognized its driver, Doc Johnson. I set down the water bucket and ran into the house through the back door to tell Mama.

She was in the kitchen, still at the table with Papa. It was something they used to do, set for a spell at the table when the meal was finished. Me and H.J. and Patsy would usually hurry through eating, anxious to do something else. Papa and Mama would sort of linger there and talk over anything they needed to settle. Lately they didn't talk, but Mama still set with Papa. She was just quiet and waiting for him to come back to her.

I ran into the room but stopped near the door, unsure of whether to say anything about the doctor in front of Papa. He might, I feared, refuse to see him.

"Mama!" I motioned for her to come to me.

She got up and crossed the room. Papa's eyes didn't even leave his half-filled plate.

"Doc's here." Excitement made my voice high. Medicine hadn't done anything for Patsy, but maybe things would be different this time. "He's coming up to the house."

Mama shot a quick look at Papa's back, and I knew she, too, was wondering if he would see the doctor. "Go invite him in. I'll tell your papa." There was determination in her voice.

Doc was coming up the porch steps when I got to the front door. My eyes went to his big black bag. Maybe there was something in there, something to bring Papa back to us. My throat was too full of hope for speaking, but I held open the screen door for him to enter.

"Morning, young lady." He put his hand on my head for just a minute as he passed by me to enter the house.

Mama was in the door between the front room and the kitchen. "Doc Johnson," she said. "Reckon my sister-in-law asked you to come about my husband." I was surprised by the sound of her voice, like she was about to cry. "He ain't been right. Not at all, since we lost the little one."

She held up her empty hands, staring at the palms.

The doctor crossed the room with sure steps. He took one of Mama's hands for just a minute, and the frightened look left her face. He has some medicine, I told myself. Doc Johnson's got some medicine to make my papa better. I turned to go out, because I knew I'd not be allowed to follow the grown-ups into the kitchen, where the doctor would examine Papa.

Outside I looked around for H.J. and was glad to see he hadn't come up from the pasture, where he'd gone right after breakfast to look for locust shells. Of course, I planned to go straight to the kitchen window for listening, and I did not want my little brother with me. The news might not be good. H.J. didn't need to hear bad news when he was up to forty on his shell collection.

I started down the porch, but my legs wouldn't go. What if the news was bad? What if I heard Doc Johnson say that there wasn't no medicine to make Papa get any better. What if Papa was just going to set there in his rocking chair and slip away to death, leaving me and Mama and H.J. all by ourselves?

Hope and fear sort of pushed at each other

inside me. Once down the porch steps, I just stood there looking around. Then I decided on the big cottonwood tree out by the front gate. It had been awhile since I'd climbed it, but I hadn't forgotten how. In a flash I jumped for the lower limb and, throwing my legs up to catch the branch, hoisted my body up to hide among the soft green leaves. I crouched there, remembering how when I was little, about H.J.'s age, I had climbed up using Papa's ladder. Then I was afraid to come down, so I stayed in the tree crying until Papa came up for me. I wanted to cry again, but the thing was I knew it would do me no good. Papa wasn't going to come to get me now even if I cried into the scary night. No medicine worked that quick.

After what seemed like a long time, Mama and Doc Johnson came out on the porch, and she walked down the steps with him. Right there under my tree they stopped to talk. I was mad. On purpose I had decided not to hear what was said, but now I couldn't help it.

Maybe I would say something or swing suddenly down between them, but I didn't. Instead I hunched there shaking, even though there was no wind to move the branches.

"I wish I could say more." Doc Johnson looked down at the ground as he spoke. "Don't know a lot about the human mind. It's a strange piece of machinery. Seems like he's just sort of turned his off because of all the misery."

Mama put her face in her hands for a minute. When she finally spoke, her voice was angry. "I know that, Doc. What I got to know is if he's coming back. Will he turn his mind back on?"

Doc looked up now. He was shaking his head with doubt and gave a little shrug of his wide shoulders. "There's just no way to tell, ma'am. Might be something will snap him out of it, sort of jerk him back all of a sudden, or could be he'll start to pull out a little at a time after the hurt eases off some." He hesitated, then went on. "And I have to say, he might just stay this way."

I gave up my hold on the tree branch and jammed my fingers into my ears. If I fell, I fell. Anything was better than hearing what Doc was saying. I closed my eyes, too, and held my breath. For some reason I counted to myself, concentrating only on the numbers and the buzz inside my head. Eventually I had to breathe, but I did not remove my fingers or open my eyes until I reached five hundred. The black Ford was gone then, and there was no sign of Mama.

I lowered myself quick to the ground, knowing what I had to do. Through the front room and into the kitchen I went as fast as I could. Papa was in his chair, but I didn't look at him. Through the back window came the sound of the pump, where Mama was finishing my job of getting water. Two fried eggs were untouched on the stove, and I grabbed them up in one fist.

"Mama," I yelled out the window. "I'm going to look for Ring." Then, before she could call back, I turned and bolted out through the house and the front door, not slowing until I was too far from the house to hear any voice calling me back.

"He sure is a pretty dog." I was talking loud and kicking up little rocks from the red dirt as I walked. "He'll be hungry. I'll put the eggs down and walk away just a space, and then he will come to eat them. Might be I can touch him this time." I knew that if I quit talking Doc's words would creep into my mind, so I kept up a steady stream of chatter to myself about the dog. When there was nothing left to say, I began to call him, making a little song of it. "Come, Ring, come, Ring, come here. That a boy, Ring, come be my dog."

·F·O·U·R·

When I got to Aunt Maybell's, there wasn't no sign of Ring. "It's daylight," I said aloud to the deserted house. "Dogs ain't out hunting with coyotes now."

I dropped down on the porch step. "Come here, Ring. Come here, boy." My voice floated out into the vacant yard and reached down toward the barn, but no black form came.

The eggs were greasy in my fist. Where should I put them? There must be a place with some sign of Ring. Holes! Old Scraps had always dug holes in the summer, some cool spot scratched out for sleeping through the scorching days.

Ring was sure to have a hole. I stood up. It could be around by the pump, where splashed-over water would make the red dirt soft for digging and cool for sleeping.

The pump was in the back, so I left the porch and made my way around the corner of the house. Stickers grabbed at my overall legs and aggravated me with their little needles. Last week the weeds with their sharp ends hadn't been everywhere.

I looked around the empty place. It was like something whispered, "They're gone," so the weeds had the nerve to grow free and so the house could start to tumble down. In no time lonesomeness would swallow up the house and land.

But I forgot about sad thoughts when I rounded the corner and saw the hole. It was right by the pump, and in the dust were traces of black dog hair! I laid down the squashed up egg.

A rusty kettle was near the hole. "I'll get you some water, Ring," I said. "Some in the pan for drinking and a dab to dampen your hole." The old pump moaned. I threw myself into it, working the handle up and down with all my might, but no water came out.

"Been too long not used." The sound of my own voice was a comfort to me. "Got to be primed."

Back behind the barn and down a little hill was a creek. If I wanted water for priming, I'd have to go down there to fetch it, but I didn't want to use the kettle. I turned it upside down over the eggs. "Shoot," I said. "I didn't hold on to them eggs all this time to have some wild thing sneak up here and swipe them while I'm gone."

In the barnyard it was easy to find an old bucket. I stood leaning against a fence post for just a short time, looking down the hill toward the creek. "Cottonmouths," I said, and the bucket shook in my hand. Water moccasins had scared me forever. "They been after me from the beginning." My voice was weak, remembering Mama's story.

I was just a baby being rocked in her arms. "Hobert," she whispered to Papa. "See what that is under the rocker. I've just about got this baby to sleep."

Papa was reading the almanac there by the lamp, and he didn't pay Mama any heed right off. "Will you look what's throwing my rocker off?" she asked again. Papa yelling woke me up, they say. Right there under Mama's chair was a young water moccasin, slithered in from the night and only stopped from finding me by Mama's rocker.

Might not be no need to prime the pump. Ring could always get his water from the creek. "Timidy, ain't she?" I repeated the words I'd heard Uncle Delbert say two years ago in the spring, when I'd slept at their house and hadn't wanted to go out into the dark for the clothes left on the line.

Aunt Maybell had stood in the door watching me so I'd not mind going, but Uncle Delbert's words had passed through the screen, making me feel sort of low until Aunt Maybell answered with "She's just young yet."

Well, I straightened my shoulders. "You're older now," I said. "Ain't no use being timidy when there ain't no one to stand in the door to watch."

With the bucket swinging from my hand, I headed toward the creek, and I started to sing. It was a song I was making up to the tune of "Onward, Christian Soldiers," but it was about Ring.

There was a trail from the barn down to the creek left over from the days when Uncle Delbert had cows, but the weeds were about to close in on the path. I sure did wish I hadn't started thinking about snakes, because I kept listening and watching for them as I walked.

The creek came from an underground spring with clear and sparkling water, not red the way it would be by the time it joined the Deep Fork and moved with the river off toward Arkansas. If Mama or even H.J. had been with me, I'd have enjoyed dipping my hot hands in the stream, maybe even taking off my heavy leftover winter shoes and wading. But I was all alone. Big old cottonwood trees and willows lined the creek bank. I started wondering if cottonmouth water moccasins laid their eggs in the water or up under the trees. I'd have to ask Mama, because Papa wouldn't be up to answering my questions. It was Papa who had told me that the cottonmouth got its name because of the white you could see when it opened its mouth. That was a sight I hoped not never to see, those terrible jaws showing white all around poison fangs!

Crouched there at the edge of the water, I lowered my bucket. A noise came from the trees across the little creek. I froze but breathed again when I realized no snake could make that much racket in the bushes. A cow maybe, but there ought not to be any cows on Uncle Delbert's place. It came again, the sound of breaking in the underbrush. Pirates maybe!

There was a story in a book at school about how a boy was taken by pirates. It was a scary thing to me, but Mama said it was likely a made-up tale and that besides the ocean where pirates were supposed to live was a long way off.

I stayed as still as my shaking insides would let me, my eyes searching the land across the narrow stream. Then a thought came to me. Might be it wouldn't be such a bad thing was I to be took by pirates. Maybe the Depression had set them to wandering just like it had Aunt Maybell and Uncle Delbert. They could be roaming around Oklahoma looking for children to steal.

If they took me, surely Papa would be sorry I was gone. Surely my papa would come to look for me. He would follow even to the ocean and fight the pirate leader for me. Then he would pick me up in his arms. We'd go home, and everything would be OK again at our place. It would be scary, but life at home was pretty scary now, too.

Just then I saw movement, and I could feel eyes looking at me from the left. I could imagine a pirate standing there with a wooden leg and a patch over his eye. Did I really want to be kidnapped? My heart was pounding. Might be I could outrun him, but I had to take one quick look first.

Moving my head took a lot of strength, and I looked right into a pair of eyes. But they didn't belong to no pirate. They were the soft eyes of a young deer, staring at me like maybe it knew me but couldn't think of my name. We didn't very often see deer up close. Papa said there weren't so many nowadays. It was a beautiful thing, sort of shaking as it peered at me. Timidy, I thought. There's a creature as timidy as me.

When it turned and flung itself back into the bushes, I was sorry. No living thing ought to go away thirsty on such a hot day. I dipped my bucket into the water and started back up the hill. "You can come drink now," I said soft. "The creek's all yours again. I'll not disturb you."

I was feeling better now. Seeing the deer was a gift. Now there might be a thing that would interest Papa. "She wasn't afraid of me at first," I'd say. Maybe Papa would tell me about some time when he was young. Maybe Papa had seen a deer up close like that when he was my age, and he'd tell me and H.J. about it.

"That's a blessed gift," Papa used to say when something happened like us seeing a tree full of red birds last Christmas. "Life is just full of blessed little gifts if a fellow is watching for them." Now I just had to remind Papa to watch for blessings.

I'd go back to the pump. I'd prime it, put some water in Ring's kettle, splash some into my mouth and onto my hot face. Then maybe Ring would come, and I'd have two gifts to tell Papa about.

I saw it long before I reached the pump. The kettle! It was overturned. I ran to it, and of course the eggs were gone. "It could of been a 'coon or a possum," I said out loud. But I knew it wasn't. Ring had been there watching as I put the eggs under the kettle. When I was gone, he had come to get them. Turning my body very slowly, I studied what my view held.

There was a washhouse, but the door was closed tight. Ring could have been behind it, though. Then I turned to an old, rusted-up Model A, Uncle Delbert's first car. Ring might be hiding there.

I inched toward the rusted-up Ford, reached out, and jerked at the door, which was half open. Nothing! Then I heard it, a sort of whine. Ring was there behind me, watching. Goose bumps of excitement covered my arm, but I didn't whirl around, just moved real slow so I wouldn't scare him none. At first I didn't see anything, but still I knew he was there. Then my eyes fell on the back porch, just high enough off the ground for him to crawl under, and there it was. A black head stuck out from the edge, and big brown eyes looked into mine.

"Ring," I said real soft. "Ring, I been looking for you." His eyes didn't move. The way he looked at me was honest and brave, not sideways and sneaky. I stepped toward him. There wasn't nowhere for him to run, no way to escape.

I didn't take another step. "I'll not fret you, Ring. One of these days you'll come to me, but I won't trap you." He put his head down like he understood my words, and like he was easy inside.

"I'll bring you something to eat tomorrow." I pointed to the kettle. "If you ain't here, I'll just leave it for you under the pan." I began to back away from him slowly. "I'll see you tomorrow, Ring. You're going to be my dog." After I turned and started to leave the backyard, I stopped and looked back, and said, "Good-bye, Ring." I thought maybe he was lonesome to hear someone call his name.

On the way home I thought about Doc's words, but they didn't upset me so much now. It had been a good morning, seeing the deer and getting so close to Ring. Maybe it would be like Doc said. Something might bring Papa back to us just right sudden like. Might be there would be a blessed gift like a big rainbow after a real huge storm, or it could be I'd find a rose rock. Papa always liked the little red sandstones shaped like flowers. I began to search the ground for one as I walked.

Back at the house H.J. was on the porch. When he saw me, he ran down the steps. "I found four more," he said. "Reckon I'll be up to fifty in just a day or two."

"That's good." I gave him a smile, and it was one I really felt. "I seen Ring," I told him. "We are going to have us a dog, Hobert Joseph Junior. We are going to have us one real fine dog."

Inside everything was still. The house seemed awful dark after the noon sun. "Mama," I called, but she didn't answer. I went out to the kitchen. Papa was in his chair. I didn't say anything to him. I wanted to talk to Mama first. Then I would come back to work on Papa.

From the bedroom I could hear crying, and my heart liked to break. Mama didn't know I was in the house. She tried so hard not to never cry when me or H.J. was around, but I knew. We would come in and find her red eyed, and I would know.

I tiptoed into the room. She was stretched across the bed with her face down. "Mama," I said, real soft like I had talked to Ring. "Mama."

She set up. "Jessie." She wiped at her eyes. "Patsy dying," she said. "That took even more from us than just that sweet little thing. When Patsy died, we lost your papa too."

"Oh, no." My voice was fierce. "We ain't lost Papa. No sir. He will come back to us, Mama. I know he will."

She set up and held out her arms to me, but this time it was me that comforted Mama.

"What would I do without you, Jessie?" she said. "What would any of us do without you?"

·F·I·V·E·

For two days I took Ring food right after breakfast. On the first it was eggs again, and on the next I carried a can full of leftover beans. He wasn't around either time. I was awful disappointed, but I left the food under his kettle, sure he wasn't far away. Maybe even watching me.

On Sunday morning I woke up early, because I had a plan concerning the fried potatoes I'd tucked away from supper the night before. Maybe Mama would let me go early. Before breakfast Ring might be there, and I could talk to him again.

Even though it wasn't nearly breakfast time, Mama was already in the kitchen. For a minute I stood in the door and watched. There was something different about the way she was, her moving around with a sort of reason to her step. She glanced up from her biscuit cutting as I came in. "We're fixing to go to camp meeting," she told me.

Camp meeting and dinner on the ground! It was my favorite thing about summer. But now it seemed part of a different lifetime, Papa helping put up the poles, me with the other kids dragging brushy limbs for the roof to keep off the sun. Maybe a freezer of ice cream. Us all laughing.

I wondered if Preacher Daniel was already there, with his camp set up beside the brush arbor. Likely this year the offering would be different. "Brothers and sisters," he'd say like always, wiping preaching sweat off his brow. "Give what the Lord leads you to share." But now he'd be lucky if folks had extra enough to invite him home for weekday supper.

Even in hard times, though, I was pretty sure there would be lemonade and fried chicken for Sunday dinner on the ground. I just didn't believe they would bother to have camp meeting dinner without lemons floating around in big stone jars and chicken cooked up golden and brown.

And there would be people, old folks talking about the good days, near-growed girls with their fellows. Everybody singing "Washed in the Blood," with maybe a baby crying in the background. The girls I went to school with would come. I hadn't seen them since Patsy died. They would look at me different. Having a dead sister would make me important. I gave my head a hard shake. It wasn't decent for me to think such a thing, like I was glad Patsy died just so I'd be up a step with Mildred and Wilma.

As a punishment to myself I wouldn't go. Besides, there was Ring. This could be the day he would be waiting for me. "I don't want to go to camp meeting," I told Mama.

She put the bread in the oven without saying anything to me, so I tried again. "Can I go on over to see about Ring now? I ain't hungry."

"Jessie." She reached out and brushed the hair out of my eyes. "We're going to camp meeting, you, me, H.J."—she paused and glanced out the window, thinking, "and maybe even your papa."

If we could just get him to go! Meeting! Music and people! It might be just what Papa needed. But I doubted that the hunched figure on the back steps could be convinced to stir. Still, there was a chance. Papa did purely love meetings and singing "Shall We Gather at the River?" for baptizing.

"No," he said when we asked him. He only said it once. Then stood up and walked into the kitchen, where he set down in the rocking chair and started the endless movement.

I looked at Mama. Her eyes were sad, but she held up her head. "We're going anyway," she told me. "And we won't go empty-handed." She reached for a big loaf of bread, baked yesterday. "I've made deviled eggs, too, and a mess of greens."

A wonderful idea hit me. "We'll walk right by Aunt Maybell's. I'll go to meeting and still leave a bite for Ring."

"You sure do put a lot of store in that dog, Jessie." She shook her head. "You might not never really tame him. He wasn't even attached to Maybell or Delbert."

"Oh, I'll tame him sure enough. You just wait and see. Ring will be our dog, and Papa will be right again." I set out dishes for breakfast.

Before we left for meeting, me and H.J. had baths in the big washtub out by the pump the way we did in summer to save hauling in buckets of water to the kitchen. When we was all ready, Mama looked at us. "We're clean," she said. "It's all God requires." She put on her straw hat, and we set out to walk the three miles to the river, where camp meetings always took place.

I was excited about dinner and about seeing my friends, but it was Ring that occupied my thoughts as we walked. There was a good little bunch of potatoes wrapped in the old newspaper I carried, and Mama had let me add some biscuits left from breakfast. I hoped we would spot him even before we got to the house, so my eyes searched the ragweed in the bar ditch and over the sunflowers and out into the fields as far as I could see.

I started calling as soon as the house came in sight. H.J. was busting to help. "Ring," he yelled, his hands cupped around his mouth. "We got food."

"Maybe you ought not to," I told him "I think he sort of knows my voice." I could see he was disappointed, so I added, "He's sure going to like you, though, real special."

We were at the pump by then. Mama set down the basket of food she carried. "Just time for a drink." We all had one from the water we cupped in our hands. Mama was itching to go, but I walked away from her. Turning my back on her impatient eyes, I called and called, but there was no sign of Ring.

She walked over to me and put her arm around

my shoulder. "I hate to see you fretting over a dog. Wild thing like that, there's just no telling."

Paying her no heed, I ran to put the potatoes under his kettle. "Here, Ring, " I said, near crying. "Come eat."

"We're going now," Mama said, and with droopy spirits I followed her out to the main road, kicking rocks as I went.

I kept my head turned, looking so hard for Ring that I didn't even hear the Cansters' worn-out truck come bumping over the hill. "Jessie." Mama had to yell and pull at my arm to get me off the road.

Red dirt filled the air around us. When I opened my eyes, the old black truck had stopped. Mr. Canster stuck his head out of the window. "Reckon you're going to camp meeting."

On the other side Mrs. Canster stepped out onto the running board and put her bonnet-covered head up over the cab. "Come crawl in alongside of me," she said to Mama. "Young ones can hop up back."

I surveyed the rear, where the two redheaded Canster boys stared out at us from the beat-up truck bed like they had never seen other human things. One was about the age of H.J., the other not much older.

Mr. Canster was out now too, looking at a tire on the back. "Needs air." He sighed.

"We got to stop every little bit," his wife explained, as he took the pump from the back.

"I'll patch it first thing tomorrow." Mr. Canster didn't like discussing the worn condition of his tires. With a scowl he attached the hose, began working the pump up and down, and changed the subject. "Been seeing to things at Delbert's, have you? Heard they was gone."

"Yes." Mama adjusted her hat and wiped dust from her face with a handkerchief. "Gone long enough now I suppose to be in California."

"We been to feed our dog," said H.J., and he started to climb up beside the Canster boys on the back.

"Your dog hanging around Delbert's?" Mr. Canster asked. There was a tone in his voice that made me feel uneasy.

"He's talking about Delbert's dog," said Mama. "The kids been feeding him some." She moved around to the other side of the truck.

"Some big dogs has took to running with coyotes around here." Mr. Canster shifted his tobacco into his cheek and spit. "I'm fixing to get some fellows, do some hunting. Maybe get rid of them pesky critters afore they start taking down stock."

"It wouldn't be Ring," I blurted out, but he just looked at me like I ought to be taught to be seen and not heard. Still, I went right on. "Ring wouldn't hurt no cows."

"You think Hobert would want to join up for a hunt one of these days?" he asked Mama as he unfastened the air pump and put it back in the truck.

"Hobert ain't been feeling so well lately," said Mama, sort of soft and sad. Mrs. Canster was out now, and I saw her pat Mama's arm in sympathy while they climbed in.

The redheaded boys didn't speak until the truck started. "My pa's got a big gun," the bigger one yelled over the rattle. He made his hand in the shape of a gun, extending the arm and pointing his finger. "Pow." He stood up and fired pretend shots at each side of the road. "Pow, pow. He'll shoot them old dogs. Coyotes too."

Just then we hit a big bump. "You better be careful," I told him. "Lots of little kids been throwed out of the back of trucks and mashed on this road, like run-over terrapins."

Nothing more was said during the rest of the trip. I hunched in the corner of the truck bed, the wind hitting my face like slaps from hot fingers and fear a rock, hard in my belly. Ring couldn't get shot. He just couldn't.

We all stood up when the truck turned off the main road onto the river trail made by the churchmen. Years ago trees had been cleared away for parking and river sand piled up to make a kind of beach where we would stand to watch the baptism.

The brush arbor was already filling up with people when we pulled up. Even before the motor stopped I jumped out and started to run over to where I saw Mildred and Wilma standing near the arbor front.

But suddenly I felt real shy, like I didn't know them none. They stood there in their best dresses and looked at me across the distance, but they didn't call to me at all. It was because Patsy was dead. Patsy's dying changed everything. Instead of feeling important like I'd expected, I just felt awful lonesome. I wanted Mama and turned to run to her.

But then Wilma came over to me. "Here." She held out her hand with a cardboard fan. HENSEN'S

GROCERY AND DRY GOODS was printed on it in big letters. The fans were a part of camp meeting, given by the merchants in town on account of them wanting folks to see their name and come in to buy. I knew Mr. Hensen wasn't hankering after our business, but I took the fan anyway. "I ain't hot," said Wilma, and she smiled.

"Thank you." I looked down, feeling better but still shy.

"Come on," called Mildred. "We want to get a seat up front so we can see what goes on if Mrs. Jenkins gets fired up and goes to shouting."

"Papa was here last night for service," Wilma told us as we walked. "Said Mrs. Jenkins done her shouting then. She don't never have strength enough to get the spirit two days in a row."

The benches were made of boards supported by fence posts drove into the ground. Mama and H.J. came down to settle in front of us. She's remembering how us girls was took with a fit of giggles last year, I thought. But she had no cause to worry about me. Giggling days seemed long gone. Maybe she knew that, though, because it was only H.J. she warned. "You behave," I heard her threaten, but even that wasn't necessary. He squirmed a bit at first, but once the preacher opened his big black Bible and started to read about Moses striking the rock to bring forth water, my little brother set up plumb straight on the edge of his bench and listened real interested like. Him acting like that, Mama would be talking again about him growing up to be a preacher.

Brother Daniel pounded on the pulpit. "Repent," he shouted, and with his burning blue eyes he searched his congregation for sinners. It came to me that Mr. Canster might be took with the love of God and decide not to shoot helpless creatures, but I didn't ever recall such a decision being made at any other meeting. A couple of people did go forward at altar call. I was glad, because Preacher had worked so hard. Overall though it was a pretty dull service, Mrs. Jenkins staying quiet, her head dropped forward in a doze.

Even with the fan I was hot and glad when Preacher cut "Just As I Am" to two verses. "He's hungry, too, I reckon," Wilma whispered into my ear, and she patted her stomach.

H.J. stayed perfectly still, gazing up front until Brother Daniel pronounced, "Let us break bread together."

Some of the big boys shouted agreement, and my little brother turned around to me. "I got a plan," he said, but Wilma pulled on me to go out and get in line.

There was a bunch of talking and backslapping as everyone moved out from under the arbor to where boards resting on sawhorses held the platters stacked high with food.

We pushed a little harder than was polite to get near the front of the line. "Brother James," said Preacher, "will you lead us in asking the Lord's blessing?"

"Prays too long." Mildred sighed. We bowed our heads, and I closed my eyes while he asked for blessing and forgiveness, but the prayer went on and on. "Lord," he was saying when I just had to sneak a look at the food, "we sure don't need no more dry weather."

Mildred and Wilma were looking too. Probably never bowed for prayer at all, I thought with disapproval. "Ain't it a sight? So much of it," Mildred whispered. We edged a little closer to the tables.

Finally, with Mr. James right in the middle of telling God how tired we all was of the Depression, someone shouted, "Amen." Mrs. Jenkins took the most important post and started serving up chicken. I kept my sights on the pile. There was plenty of it. Did I dare take two drumsticks? Mama was way to the back of the line and wouldn't see, but Mrs. Jenkins wasn't smiling at no one. I figured her nap hadn't been long enough. Still, when my turn came, I put my hand out quick, snatching up two legs. She saw me, grunted disapproval, and swatted in the direction of my wrist with her meat turner. No matter. I just didn't look at her. If she wanted to stop me from getting one for Ring and one for me, she'd have to wrestle me down and take them away from me. "Greedy," she muttered, but I kept my free hand over the chicken and moved out of her reach to the berry cobbler.

We didn't have no quilt like the grown-ups was spreading for setting, but we found a nice shady rock big enough for all three of us. I was too busy eating to notice who spread out nearby until I heard his voice. At first he talked about the weather and corrected the two redheads for eating too fast; still, my appetite sort of died down just at the sound of him.

"Hey, Hank," he said then to a fellow on the other side of him. "How about you and me going out this evening? Thinning out them coyotes and dogs? They'll be after your new calf, I wager."

"Never knowed a coyote to jump stock. Now, wild dogs, they're a different story. Reckon you're right. It's time to do something about them."

Then Mr. Canster went off into a story about a coyote hunt him and his papa had when he was just a little sprout, but I didn't listen. The drumstick dropped from my fingers back onto my plate, and I stared up at the tree's limbs above me. "Ain't you going to eat that chicken?" Mildred rolled her eyes. Wasting food was a bigger sin than any of the ones Brother Daniel had preached against.

"I'll eat it sure," I said. "Saving it for later." Looking around to make sure Mama wasn't there to fuss about grease, I wrapped the meat in my good white handkerchief and hid the bundle in my pocket.

There was no use to say a word about Ring to Wilma or Mildred. They might understand my school secrets, like how I thought Howard Dickerson was sweet on me last year, but there just wasn't no way to tell anyone how important that black dog was or that he was the only thing that gave me hope.

While the other girls finished their meal, I sipped lemonade from my cup and studied the cottonwood tree above my head. I won't think about it, I told myself. I'll just think about the leaves and that ladybug crawling along the limb.

Finally we gathered on the banks of the muddy river for baptizing. I was careful to make sure we weren't nowhere near Mr. Canster, because I didn't want to remember anything he had said and because I didn't reckon it was decent to stand beside a body and hate him whilst singing hymns.

Preacher waded down till the muddy water came up close to his middle. First we sang "Shall We Gather at the River?" I put back my head and belted out the words, sort of crawling up into the sound of voices around me and blocking out the mean pictures of men with guns that tried to creep into my mind.

Then Preacher held up his hand. "Our Lord his ownself was baptized," he said.

Ordinarily, I'd have been real interested in the service. Jake Johnson, who was wanting to court Wilma's big sister, was first in line. "He's just doing this on account of Mama not wanting Mary Beth seeing no boy that ain't been dunked," Wilma giggled. "Hope he drowns."

Just then Mama kind of eased her way through

the crowd to where we was. "You seen H.J?" she asked.

With my hand, I shaded my eyes from the sun that threatened to set my hair to blaze and looked around. There wasn't no sign of my little brother, but I knew when I saw the fingers. And I saw them before someone shouted, "Look!"

A hand was rising up out of the water right near the preacher. "It's Satan," screamed Mrs. Jenkins. "Come to stop the baptism."

"Sakes alive," moaned Mama, knowing it wasn't Satan at all. She started to wade right into the river.

Either Brother Daniel knew, too, or else he didn't even fear the devil, because he reached down where we had seen the hand, and out of the red water he pulled up H.J. wearing nothing but dripping underdrawers.

Mrs. Jenkins screamed again like she couldn't tell a waterlogged six-year-old from Satan. Lots of people were hooting with laughter.

"I aimed to come up over there." H.J. pointed to a group of little trees growing into the water's edge a few feet away.

"Get your pants on, Hobert Joseph Harper Junior. You get your pants on this instant." He ran up the bank and headed for the trees. Mama was close behind.

Preacher held up his hands to quiet down the crowd. "Let us continue the Lord's work," he said. The service went right on, but it sure wasn't so solemn.

"Best baptism we ever had," a man beside me grunted, but his wife jabbed him in the ribs.

"I seen you in your unders," said the littlest Canster when we was loaded for the trip home.

"So?" H.J. stuck out his lower lip. "I got cooled off. Cooler than you, I reckon." He folded his arms across his chest, daring the redhead to say another word.

The truck bumped off, and I waved to Wilma, who hadn't got loaded up yet. My hand was on my pocket, touching the chicken legs. Ring would have a full stomach tonight. Two big drumsticks. Maybe he would just stay under the porch. Maybe he wouldn't be out nosing around with coyotes in the dark.

How many hours until dark? I studied the sky as we bumped along. Four maybe. The heat suddenly seemed worse. There were traces of manure in the truck bed, and the smell began to mix with the fear inside me. I felt sick, like I might start to puke.

When Mr. Canster stopped the truck for tire airing near Aunt Maybells, I climbed out with H.J. right behind me. "We're going to get off here. Be on directly," I said through Mama's window.

She didn't protest, so I started to run. H.J. was behind me, but I didn't slow down for him. Ring might be there now. He might be right there by his kettle waiting for me.

But he wasn't. "Ring," I called. "Please, Ring. Come, boy." We looked everywhere, under the porch, in the washhouse and old car. We even went down by the creek to call, but there wasn't no dog to be seen.

It was getting late. The potatoes from morning were gone, but Ring would still be hungry. "Maybe we ought to go," I said finally. "He could be out there waiting for us to leave. Don't want him going off hunting. Not tonight."

I started to put the chicken under the kettle. "Run back down to the creek," I said to H.J. "I got a feeling he might be there. You call me do you see him. You call me right off." It was an excuse, because I wanted to be by myself.

With great care I placed the drumsticks beneath the pan. Then I got down on my knees to pray. Trying to make my voice sound like Preacher's, I said, "Lord, protect my dog. Protect him from men with guns. In Jesus' name I pray. Amen."

I stood up feeling some better. "Come on," I yelled to H.J. "Let's head for home."

I walked backwards until we was too far away to see anything near the pump. H.J. found an old can beside the road, and we took to kicking it, running to see who could boot it first. Even with me trying, H.J. beat me some. The fear churning away inside me took a lot of my strength.

"I'm wored out," I finally said, and we slowed down, deserting the can on the road.

"You know what?" H.J. asked. "I got me a plan. Preacher told about how Moses got water out of rock just by whopping it with a stick." His voice was full of excitement. "Well, there is a slew of rocks down in the south pasture. First thing tomorrow I'm getting me a stick." He stretched out his arms to show how long. "A great big one. Then I aim to go down into that pasture and make us one great big swimming hole."

Even with the fear stirring inside me, I laughed. I laughed real loud.

·S·I·X·

The night was terrible, coming to settle around me with threatening shadows and hateful sounds. When sleep finally found me, I fell into a dream about being chased by the red-headed Canster boys with knives. It was dark in the dream, me running hard. I stumbled over something. Then it was light, and I saw that what had made me fall was Papa, dead on the ground beside a lifeless Ring.

The sound of my own crying woke me up. Outside my window there was a flash of lightning and a rumble of thunder. Rain hit the roof fast and strong. A thunderstorm. I remembered Brother James's prayer about dry weather. Maybe God had heard him and me too. What time was it? How long had it been raining? Long enough to keep hunters indoors? From the living room, Grandma's clock answered me with one chime.

One o'clock! The hunt would be long over. But when had it started to rain? I could find out by going out into the night to feel the ground or look for puddles.

At the front door I stood peering through the screen, pushing myself to step out into the dark. "Timidy. Ain't she?" I said the words out loud, trying to shame my cowardly legs to movement.

You've got to know, don't you? Go on. Slowly I pushed open the screen, closing it gently so as not to wake anyone. I moved across the porch, noticing for the first time how the boards creaked.

At the bottom of the step, I kneeled and touched the grass. It was wet, but the ground beneath wasn't hardly damp at all. "Oh, Lord." I sobbed. "You didn't answer my prayer, did you? You didn't make it rain soon enough. Not soon enough to do me and Ring any good."

Papa's old shirt that I slept in was soaking wet, and so was my hair, but I ignored that, and after I went back in I stayed by the door staring out into the dripping blackness. If only I had the nerve to just go over there right now and look for him. Ring might be safe and dry under his porch. Or could be he was out there somewhere dead like in my dream. Anyway, I was terrified of the night even without a thunderstorm.

A great roll of thunder shook the house. "Jessie?" It was Mama's voice. "Where are you?"

"Here, Mama." I was thinking real quick. "I just got up to close the door." I gave it a push and ran back to bed, afraid she would find me wet. I could hear her moving around the house, shutting windows. She came to my door.

"Go back to sleep, honey. Storm won't hurt you."

I didn't say anything, just breathed easy and slow like I was already sleeping to keep her from coming over to kiss me.

After Mama was gone, I started to cry, my face in the pillow to soften the sounds. When there wasn't no more tears to come out, the sound of rain on the roof seemed like me still crying. I laid there all that night listening and looking at the blackness out my window. Finally a sort of gray light came, but the sun never did poke through the clouds.

After first light I went off to sleep for a while. Mama came to wake me for breakfast. My legs felt funny when I stood up, sort of achy and weak, and my head hurt something fierce. One bite of egg sent me running out the back door to throw up. Mama had to help me back into the house because the porch kept seeming to move under me.

"Back to bed," she said, and I wasn't too dizzy to notice that she was scared, afraid I was going to die.

"I ain't that sick, Mama," I told her when I was settled in bed. "Not like Patsy."

"Of course not, child." She set down on my bed, her hand on my forehead. "It's just a touch of summer complaint. Couple of days you'll be just fine."

The rain lasted all day and so did the whirling in my dizzy head. Between naps I would stare at my window and try to keep it from moving up and down on the wall.

All the time my mind was filled with fear that was a worse sickness than the one that owned my body. There wasn't no way I could find out about Ring today. I couldn't keep nothing down except the root tea Mama had me drink every couple of hours. When the gray day was beginning to slip into night, Mama brought in more tea and a slice of warm bread spread with melted butter. "Try this now, Jessie. Your stomach might be settled some."

She broke the bread into pieces and handed

them to me one at a time where I sat on the edge of the bed sipping tea. "Think it's going to stay down?"

I nodded my head. "I'll be all right by tomorrow."

"You're fretting over that dog, ain't you?"

"He said he was going to shoot them." I didn't want to start crying, because my head was still pounding. "That stupid Mr. Canster, going around shooting other folks' dogs."

Mama took the cup from me, set it down on the floor, and pulled me over to lean against her. "So much hurt in this old world," she said real soft. "So much hurt and no way for a mother to spare her young ones. There just ain't no way in this old world." She let me go and stood up. "The next world, though, they say that one's better."

I did feel stronger in the morning, but Mama wouldn't hear of me going over to Aunt Maybell's. "Afternoon. That'll be soon enough. What's done is done. You can go after you've had another meal in you and kept it down." She didn't even look up from her quilting, and I knew there wasn't no use to argue.

At dinner I attacked the fried okra and black-eyed peas like my stomach wasn't still feeling pretty weak. Mama was watching what I ate real close. "See," I told her. "I'm just fine." I got up from the table to leave.

"Wait for me," H.J. begged.

"Well." I hesitated. "I was sort of planning to go this time by myself." If I found Ring dead, I didn't want H.J. there. If I found Ring dead, I had to be alone when I buried him.

"No." Mama was firm. "You take your brother or you don't go. Girl been as sick as you has got no business going off that far, and you ain't going alone."

So we started off together. The hard rain had left cooler air and red mud. We had to step careful to keep from having our feet completely covered. The ground will be soft for grave digging, I thought. Then I hated myself for such. Ring was alive. He just had to be, else how was I going to go on.

I didn't even call him as we got close to the house. Fear was so big in my throat that I couldn't open up my mouth. H.J. knew, and he was real still, too, and sort of drawed up.

Ring wasn't nowhere to be seen. The kettle

was still turned upside down. Maybe the wind just blew it back like that, I told myself. Maybe I would lift it and see that the chicken was gone because Ring got it, but I was too weak, too afraid to look. "H.J." I wanted to sound like it wasn't important. "Run over and lift up the kettle." I followed, but instead of watching him, I just leaned on the pump and looked down at the mud on my shoes.

"It's still there. The chicken ain't been touched."

My stomach turned over like I was going to start throwing up again. "Put the pan back," I told him. "Ring didn't come in on account of the storm, but I reckon he'll be here today."

"Do you think he got shot?"

"No." I said it real slow, trying hard to believe my own words. "He most certainly did not get shot. That fool Canster man probably couldn't hit the broad side of a barn with no gun."

We walked back to the front of the house, and I dropped down on the front steps.

H.J. didn't sit beside me. He was still looking all around. "Do you want me to go see down by the creek?"

"It couldn't hurt, I guess, but likely Ring is off

hunting somewhere, following a jackrabbit." I watched my little brother bound off. Then, leaning against the porch post, I tried praying again.

"Lord," I said. "Ring ain't dead, is he? Please don't let Ring be dead. He wouldn't hurt no calves. I just know he wouldn't do that. He's got good, honest eyes. In Jesus' name I pray. Amen. And oh, yes, I'm awful sorry for my sins." I wished I'd have listened closer to Brother Daniel. Maybe then I would have known some particular sin to bring up that might please God.

H.J. came back up the hill with less bounce in his walk than when he went off. "We'll come back tomorrow," I told him. "Best bring food, too, because I'm just double dog certain Ring will be here waiting for us."

Neither of us talked on the way home. H.J. picked a bouquet of sunflowers for Mama, but I didn't go into the kitchen with him to give them to her. My legs were plumb tuckered out, so I just went right in to bed.

Later Mama brought something in for me to eat, but I pretended to be asleep again. I was too afraid she would try to talk to me about Ring.

✿

The next morning my body felt better, but my insides were just in pieces. I looked in the mirror over Grandma's chiffonnier. "Look," I told that girl. "You go over there today, and if he ain't there you know he's off dead somewhere. Like Mama says, there's just a bunch of hurt in this old world."

Right after breakfast we set off. I didn't even try to keep H.J. from going along. He might as well be in on the hurting, I thought. Mama was right. There ain't no way to spare him.

It was a good thing he was along. I might have missed it. H.J.'s eyes were real sharp, and it was him that seen the blood. When we turned off the main road, he was walking off a ways. "Look," he yelled, and he dropped down on his knees.

"It's blood," I said. "Sure enough." There it was, drops forming a little trail, out of the trees, through the edge of the yard, and down toward the barn.

"Is it Ring?" H.J. was holding on to my arm.

"Don't know." My whole body was shaking. "But if it is, he's alive. Dead dogs don't leave trails of blood." For a minute I just stood there, not able to move.

It was H.J. that started. "Come on," he said.

We moved toward the barn, still seeing the blood, then down the trail to the creek.

Halfway down the hill I spotted it. The black form was there in the water's edge. "Ring!" There was no movement. "He's dead," I whispered, but somehow my feet kept running.

H.J. was there first, but he waited, looking at me for direction. I dropped beside the body and put my hand out to rest on his side. The black head did not rise. The eyes did not open. H.J. started to say something, but I hushed him. For just a few seconds we were still as a picture. But then I was sure, sure enough of the slight rising and falling under my hand. "He's breathing," I said real quiet. "Oh, Ring, you're still alive."

With our fingers we parted the thick, bur-filled hair until we found the hole in his leg. "The bullet went through," I said, lifting the leg gently and putting my face on down to see the other side.

"Why's he so sick then?" H.J. had big tears running down his round cheeks.

"We got to get him home to Mama. Mama, she'll know what to do. Mama can fix him up."

"How?" He was shaking his head. "That's a awful big dog."

I stood up, my mind racing. "The barn. Maybe there will be something there." I bent to touch the dog's head. "We'll be right back, Ring. We'll take care of you, boy."

"God," I prayed as we ran. "You been answering my prayers. Now just let me find a way. Please, Lord, let me find a way."

The answer was right inside the old barn, just over in one corner. A wheelbarrow, rusty and wobbly but still usable. H.J. saw it at the same time as me. We both let out a whoop. He grabbed out the old box which was in it, and I pulled the wheelbarrow to the door.

"We got to hurry," I told him. "There wasn't much life in him." At first I tried to run down the hill pushing the wheelbarrow in front of me, but the bumps were too bad. "Don't want to tear the wheel off," I said and slowed down.

H.J. ran on ahead and was kneeling beside Ring when I got there.

"You got to help me lift him." I studied the dog. "You take the rear in case he comes to. He might bite."

"I ain't scared." H.J. walked over to touch Ring's head.

Very gently we lifted the big dog between us.

He filled the wheelbarrow with some of him sticking over both ends. Before we moved I checked again for breathing. "Still alive," I announced. "Don't you die." I stroked his head. "Just don't you die now."

"He won't," said H.J. "We got us a dog now for sure."

·S·E·V·E·N·

Getting up the hill was the hardest part. I walked backwards, pulling. H.J. was at the other end trying to push the wheelbarrow and steady Ring too. We were both sweating pretty bad by the time we got to the barn, but neither one of us said anything about going to the pump for water.

After the hard hill I was hoping the mile of road that separated us from home would seem sort of easy, but it didn't. We had to stop and clean the mud that collected on the wheels. At first we tried scraping it with sticks. Then we just went to using our hands. The sun beat down, and water left in holes after the big rain seemed to rise up and make the air pure steam. When we had to stop to rest, I'd check Ring to see if he was still alive.

At last the house came in sight. "Run on ahead," I told H.J. "Tell Mama. We got to put him in the calf lot. Else he might run away when he's stronger." I looked down at the still form. It seemed foolish to believe the dog could live, but still there was hope. Maybe Mama would know what to do.

H.J. shot off to the house. I started talking to Ring. "My papa's sick too," I told him. "But when you're both better you can go hunting together. I'll brush all them old burs out of your coat too. Folks will be talking about how pretty you are."

I had the wheelbarrow almost to the calf pen when Mama came running out with H.J. She looked down at Ring. "Oh, Jessie." She was shaking her head. "Are you sure he's still alive?"

"Feel." I reached for her hand and pulled it down to the dog. "He is, ain't he?"

"Just barely. Poor thing's eaten up with infection." She pushed back the hair from the bullet hole. "Sore's full of pus and fever."

"You can fix him, can't you?" H.J. pulled on Mama's skirt. "Can't you?"

"We'll try." She looked right into my eyes. "But you got to promise not to get your hopes too high."

Promising did no good. My hopes was high. "Live. Live." The plea kept going through my mind as Mama and me moved Ring from the wheelbarrow into the calf shed.

H.J. went with her back to the house to get things, but I stayed, stroking the black fur and talking to him. "We'll take care of you, boy. Good old boy. Good old Ring."

When they came back H.J. carried a bottle of water and a rag, Mama a basket. First I held his mouth open while Mama poured in a bit of water. His eyes flickered open, and my hopes soared.

Then Mama cut the hair away from the wound and poured in peroxide. Ring opened his eyes again and whimpered a little. "Stings, don't it, boy?" I said. "I don't ever like it none either, but it makes us better."

"I'll make a poultice now," said Mama. "It's all there is left to do."

"How about some milk? I could squeeze drops of milk down his throat. Might give him some strength." I was up ready to go for the milk.

"Couldn't do any harm, I don't suppose." Mama gave me a little smile. "Just remember what I said about your hopes."

All day I stayed near Ring. Mama didn't say nothing about my chores, but she did make me come in for supper. Papa was in the rocking chair.

I felt bad, because I hadn't been thinking about my papa much for the last few days. When no one else was in the room, I went over to him.

Reaching out to stop his rocking, I said, "Papa. Papa, it's me, Jessie. I love you, Papa. You are going to be well again, and so is Ring. I'm going to have my papa back, and I'm going to have me a dog." He looked at me, and for a minute I thought he was going to say something. Instead he started to rock again, but I thought it was a good sign. He had heard me, and he was interested. I wouldn't say anything to Mama, not yet. Still, I felt good.

Even after it got dark I stayed with Ring. "See," I told him, "I ain't so timidy when I'm with you. You and me, we are going to take care of each other."

H.J. was already asleep. Mama came out to set on the back step. I knew she was there, but I wasn't going to leave Ring until she called and said I had to. Instead of calling, she walked down to the calf lot and leaned against the post.

I was still on the ground near Ring. "You're going to need a good washing before bed tonight," she said. "Better get up to the house and get started."

Suddenly I was awful tired. Bed sounded so good, but I wanted Mama to say something first. "He's better." I pulled myself up and went over to her. "He opened his eyes some." I reached out to touch Mama's arm. "Ring will be OK. You think so too, now. Don't you?"

"Mercy, child, you smell like dog. I'll heat you some water." She took my arm and sort of guided me toward the house.

Mama talked about bathwater and how the rain had been good for the garden, but I didn't say nothing else. There wasn't nothing to say. She still believed Ring would die.

But I didn't. When the house was quiet, I got up from bed and went to a window. "I'm here," I whispered out toward the calf lot. "I am here to take care of you."

His eyes were open when I first saw him before breakfast the next morning. "Mama! H.J.!" I ran back into the house. "Milk. I think Ring could lap some milk."

Mama beat up an egg to go in the milk, and her and H.J. both followed me back out. I poured the milk in the saucer and put it right beside his head.

"That's one of my good dishes," Mama protested.

"Shush," I said like she was H.J., and she let me get away with it. We were all quiet, watching Ring. He lifted his head just a little, stuck out his tongue, and lapped at the milk. Then he put his head down and closed his eyes.

"That a boy!" I yelled. Me and H.J. locked arms and started to dance. Even Mama was laughing.

We slowed, and I grabbed at Mama's dress sleeve. "He's going to live. He is! Say it!"

"Well, it looks like there's a real good chance. A real good chance."

"Whoopee!" yelled H.J. "I'm fixing to build a doghouse!"

In the afternoon I helped can some corn, but Mama had to tell me every little thing to do. My mind was just all took up with Ring.

That evening H.J. went with me out to the lot to take the milk. When we bent down over Ring, he growled and showed his teeth. H.J. jumped back. "Why'd he do that? Why'd he want to bite us?"

"Oh, he don't mean to hurt us." Very slowly

and carefully I scooted the saucer over closer to his head. "He's just hurt and confused."

"Like Papa?" H.J.'s face was sad.

"That's right," I said. "That's right. Ring and Papa are an awful lot alike. They been hurt, down deep. But they're both good. And they will both heal."

"You think so?"

I put my hands on my little brother's shoulders and turned him to face me. "I know so, but, H.J., don't say a word to Mama about the growl." I tightened my grip on his shoulders. "Not a word. She'd go fussing about Ring being dangerous."

"I won't tell."

"Just let me do the tending to him for a while. When it don't hurt so much, he'll come around and be friendly. I bent down just enough to pour the milk into the dish.

What I had to do was keep Mama away from Ring until the hurting stopped. "I'll put the poultice on him my own self," I told her when we went back to the house. "He's my dog. It ought to be me going to all the trouble."

"Lord knows I've got enough to do, but you be careful getting that poultice hot. Don't burn yourself." Mama went back to her quilting, and I was relieved.

How long, I wondered, would it take for Ring to quit hurting? My eyes fell on my father, rocking away in the chair. Well, hadn't he looked at me just yesterday like he was going to speak to me? I walked over to him. "Papa," I said. "Papa, we got us the best dog. I'll bet you he's a dandy hunting dog." He didn't look at me, and I walked away. But when I turned back for another glance, he was watching me. "Remember the squirrels we used to eat? They sure was good." I thought I saw some interest in his eyes. "Ring's a blessed gift," I added.

For three days Ring was a little stronger each time I saw him, holding his head up just a bit better each time. Sometimes he growled, but sometimes he didn't, just watched me, trying to understand what had happened to him and to figure if any of it was my fault.

I talked to him lots and lots. There on the ground in the calf pen, I'd pull up grass and make little piles of it while I told Ring all about everything. "My little sister Patsy died," I explained.

"And Papa just sort of slipped away from us. See, things had been real hard before that, too, no money for nothing. It just broke Papa to pieces watching Patsy die, him not able to do nothing to stop it. But Papa loves me too, and H.J. and Mama. He'll come back to us, Ring. One of these days, likely just when we need him most, Papa will come back to us. He will. My papa will come back to us just when we need him most."

On the fourth morning I took Ring some left-over eggs and biscuits after breakfast. He was partly up, his front legs straight. Real slow and easy I walked over to him and put the food down in front of him. Then he started trying to stand, his body shaking with the strain.

My eyes never left Ring, so I didn't know that Mama had come in the gate behind me until she was there beside me. Ring turned his head toward us, and a great growl came from down deep in his chest. "Stop it," yelled Mama. Then he lunged at her snapping at her leg before he fell.

"Ring." I stepped toward him, but Mama jerked at my arm.

"No!" She pulled me with her toward the lot entrance. "Injured wild thing. Too dangerous for a child to mess with." She fastened the gate after us.

"Mama." I was crying. "You just scared him. He wouldn't hurt me. Ring wouldn't never hurt me."

Her voice was low and steady, the way it was when there wasn't no use to argue with her. "Jessie, you ain't going around that dog. Big as he is, he could kill a girl like you. You're not to go back inside that pen." I was sobbing. "Do you hear me, Jessie Harper?"

I heard her, but I didn't say so. Instead I turned and ran. I ran fast, until I was down in the pasture out of sight of the house. Then I dropped in a heap under a blackjack tree to cry.

The sun was high in the sky before I decided to go back. I'd talk to her, I planned. I wouldn't cry or get excited. I'd just talk real reasonable and grown-up like. "Mama," I'd say. "You come out right at the wrong time. He was hurting from trying to get up. All that pain going through him and him seeing you at the same minute. He thought it was you caused it. Ring ain't bad, Mama. I know Ring ain't bad."

I didn't get to say any of it, though. Mama was in the kitchen canning corn again. "This canning's got to get done. Come winter there won't be much to eat around here besides eggs." I knew it was a bad decision, me running off and leaving my chores.

Washing up real careful, I went over to help her. I was reaching for some jar lids when she said it. "Jessie, I'm going to take your papa's gun and shoot the dog. It's the only decent thing to do."

The jar rings went out of my hands to the floor, rattling and rolling off under the stove. "Shoot him?" I stared at her, wanting to believe I hadn't understood her words.

"Him the way he is. That leg ain't ever going to be right, and he's got too much misery inside to be any good to anyone." She turned back to the canning like we was through talking.

My eyes went out the window to Papa on the back porch. "Are you going to shoot Papa too?" I spit the words at her. "Are you, Mama? He's just as hurt as Ring is. If you shoot Ring, why you might as well shoot Papa too!"

She reached out and pulled me to her, but I held myself tight, not leaning into her any. "Honey," she said. "I'd spare you this if I could."

I stepped back. "You don't think Papa is going to get any better, do you? Tell me true, Mama."

Her face was white, and her eyes were big, but

dry. "We got to get along without him, Jessie. We got to learn, and you got to give up that wild dog."

"I can't, Mama." I walked to the door. "I can't get along without Papa, and I can't let you shoot Ring."

At supper I didn't say a word to Mama or to H.J. I knew she hadn't told him about what she was thinking to do to Ring, else he'd be crying. Likely she was planning to wait till H.J. was asleep. Then she'd make up some story about how Ring got away in the night.

Well, maybe he would. I filled my plate, but I didn't set down. Instead I carried the beans and potatoes out to the calf pen, opened the gate, and scrapped the food just outside the opening.

"Come here, boy," I called. "Come get it." I watched as he pulled himself up and wobbled over to eat. Then I turned and walked away. I didn't look back or say good-bye to my dog.

Inside Mama and H.J. were still at the table with Papa. "Mama," I said. "You just can't shoot Ring." She looked at H.J. and put her finger to her lips to hush me, but I ignored her. "Please,

Mama. I left the gate open. Give him a chance to go off in the woods."

She looked down at her plate. "It ain't the kind thing to do. He'll just crawl out there to die."

I went over to her, kneeled on the floor, and put my head in her lap. "Please, Mama. Please give him a chance."

She stroked my hair. "It ain't something I relish doing, shooting a creature like that."

"You won't do it, will you?" H.J. came to lean against her, crying.

"No," she said. "If he can get away, we'll just let him go." We stayed there, and all three of us cried. There was just so much to cry over.

·E·I·G·H·T·

Ring got away. I could see in the dust where he had fell down a couple of times. Then he was on the grass of the pasture, and I couldn't tell what happened after that.

It was August, the hottest month of all. School would be starting before long. Country schools started near the end of August because of a break in fall for cotton picking. Maybe this year would be different. Lots of folks didn't even plant cotton because the price was so low. None of that mattered to me. We didn't have no cotton. We didn't have a dog either, or a papa that was really with us. Me and H.J. didn't have anything to care about. He had even quit collecting locust shells.

Mama kept working. I knew what happened with Ring wasn't her fault really, and I knew she was awful sorry. Neither one of us said anything about it. Even H.J. never mentioned that we had a dog for a while, and he tore down the doghouse he had been working on.

Just one thing caused a little flutter of exitement. A letter came one day from Aunt Maybell. Inside the envelope was a folded piece of paper and two picture postcards. Mama read the letter out loud. Me and H.J. listened, but Papa just kept rocking.

California wasn't so great, according to Aunt Maybell, and times weren't much better for her and Uncle Delbert there than they had been at home. She said she reckoned even Uncle Delbert had about had his fill and that they'd likely be coming back to their place as soon as they could get ahead enough money for gasoline.

The two picture postcards were for me and H.J. One was a picture of a bright-colored desert and the other of mountains. The desert had H.J.'s name on the back of it, and the mountains had mine. "This is pretty country," wrote Aunt Maybell underneath my name, "but I miss the red dirt, and I miss my Red-dirt Jessie."

I knew Aunt Maybell was reminding me to be strong, but I wasn't sure there was fight left in me. I put the postcard up in the edge of the mirror on Grandma's chiffonier, and I looked at it some when I walked by.

The days got hotter and the grasshoppers seemed to be everywhere, finishing off our garden and starting on the hollyhocks.

"At least the chickens like to eat the things," Mama said about the grasshoppers when she came back from the garden with an empty basket. "Thank the Lord for the chickens. We can even fry up a few of the young ones come fall."

It was like Mama saying that about the chickens was bad luck. Like a person shouldn't ever say anything good without knocking on wood.

It happened that very night. The house was quiet and dark, me in bed staring at my window, feeling lonesome and miserable. Outside I could hear coyotes howling in the distance. I started thinking about Ring. Could he be out there with them? Likely he was dead for sure. There hadn't been no more sign of him at Aunt Maybell's.

Then the sound changed. It was the short, quick yelping of close-up coyotes and suddenly the squawking of chickens. They was in the henhouse! Thieving coyotes in our henhouse. My mouth was open to yell, but I closed it without making a sound. Ring! Ring might be out there too! I had to see.

Not even thinking about being afraid, I jumped up and ran. Through the living room, around the house to the chicken house, barely noticing the stickers in my feet, but reaching down to pick up some small rocks.

I hurled the rocks at the henhouse, then tore into the door. Two dark forms, not big enough for Ring, were there, but they ran through the tumbled-down back wall, the part Papa had used for Patsy's grave box and never fixed. One coyote dragged one of Mama's hens in its mouth. I followed them, heaving rocks, but they were way too fast for me.

"Blasted coyotes." I should of woke up Mama. She wasn't that good with Papa's gun, though, couldn't hit no moving target.

"No." I whispered it to myself as I crept back into the house. "It's Papa that's got to help. Them coyotes won't come back tonight. Tomorrow I'll tell Papa. He'll help us, because he's got to. We can't get along without chickens."

I climbed back into bed. "Papa will come back to us just when we need him most." I repeated to myself what I had said to Ring.

The next morning at breakfast Mama looked awful bad. "Sick headache," she said. "You'll have to clean up, Jessie."

"She's sick with worry," I said to Papa when she had left the room. "She's just plumb sick with worry." I bent beside his chair and took his face in my hands. "Do you hear me?" The eyes that looked back at me were empty.

Turning back to the stove, I slammed down the hot water kettle onto the burner. He wasn't going to help us. Mama was right. We had to learn to get along without Papa. I was ashamed of how I'd been moping around, leaving all the work and worry to Mama. Well, I'd fix the henhouse wall, and until it was done, I'd guard the chickens. *In the dark night?* a voice in my head asked.

Well, there was someone to help me. I went to the back door. "H.J.," I called. "Come here. We got to make us a plan." I stood in the door and watched him running toward me. "You and me, H.J.," I told him. "We got to get to work."

"Ain't no boards here for fixing that," said H.J. when we went out to study the chicken house wall.

"There's some in Uncle Delbert's barn." I started toward the calf lot. "We'll have to use the wheelbarrow again."

It wasn't easy, making three trips to get the boards. Between loads, we'd go in to check on Mama . She was too sick to even ask what we were up to. Papa, of course, didn't say nothing either.

My feet was aching, and my legs didn't feel like they could carry me another step when we got back with the last load. I dumped it with the other wood. "First thing tomorrow, we'll start nailing."

"I know how," said H.J. "I learned a bunch when I was making—" He stopped. "I learned a bunch about nailing." Me and H.J. never talked about Ring. There just wasn't nothing to say.

"That's right." I hit my overall legs to knock out the dust. "Tomorrow we nail, but tonight we got to guard them chickens. We can't afford to lose another single one to the thieving coyotes."

"We going to guard the henhouse in the night?" H. J.' s eyes were big.

"Yes, sir, but not a word to Mama." I started

toward the house. "Right now we got to heat up some black-eyed peas for supper. Maybe I'll make some corn bread. Guards need lots of strength."

Talking brave to H.J. was easy, but when evening started moving in, with whippoorwills singing their night songs and an owl hooting off down behind the barn, I didn't feel so confident.

Mama's head had eased some, and she worked on her quilt by the lamplight.

"Want to play some checkers?" H.J. already had the board, and we spread it on the kitchen table. "When do we go?" he whispered as we put the checkers out, but I shook my head for him to be quiet.

I wasn't hard to beat, because my eyes were on the windows, and my mind was on dark forms that would come in the night. Coyotes don't never bother people, I reminded myself, but still my insides felt cold.

"It's bedtime, I reckon," Mama finally said, and she led Papa by the hand to their room, coming back to say good night to me and H.J. and to put out the lamps.

"When the clock strikes ten," I said. "Meet me at the front door. Don't go to sleep now."

"I won't," he promised, shaking his head. But

I wasn't so sure. It had been a full day for a six-year-old, and his eyes looked real tired.

For my own self, there was no danger of slipping off. My heart was pounding in my chest louder that the sound of the clock when it finally did begin to strike ten. "You could still tell Mama," I said as I put my feet down on the floor, but I wouldn't. It was time to put the timidy girl behind me.

Carrying my shoes, I padded across the living room floor. Should of told H.J. to bring his shoes too. We don't want to be slowed by stickers. He'll have to go back to get them. But my little brother wasn't at the door.

He's asleep, I thought. Leave the poor little kid alone, the voice said inside my head. He's tuckered. Let him sleep.

I stood there looking out the door into the night. There was a big moon, plenty of light. "Nothing to be afraid of," I whispered. But I couldn't open the screen. I just couldn't. With H.J. to watch I had to act brave. Without him I couldn't even make myself go outside.

He slept in a tiny nook off the living room, right near Mama and Papa. I'd have to be mighty quiet rousing him. Very carefully, I moved across the floor to his bedside. With my hand over his mouth I shook him. He was easier than I thought to wake up, and I could see that he remembered right off why I was there.

With my finger to my lips I began to move, motioning for him to follow. Then I remembered and looked around for his shoes, hardly worn since winter. "Get your shoes," I whispered, and he pulled them from under the bed.

When we were outside, we set down on the porch steps to put on our shoes. "They're sort of little," said H.J.

"Can you run in them?" I reached over to tie the laces for him.

"Sure," he said. "I can run."

"Well, you might as well get used to being cramped," I advised. "It ain't likely there will be any new ones this winter."

"Where we going now?" He scooted close to me.

"There ain't nothing to be afraid of," I told him, hoping he couldn't hear the pounding of my heart. "I guess we'll go out and settle in the weeds near the chicken house." I held up my hand to the breeze. "Good, wind's from the right direction. Coyotes might not smell us."

"Wish we had Papa's gun." H.J. stood up. "I'd shoot me some coyotes."

"We got no business trying to shoot a gun. Don't you know what Papa says about kids touching guns? Tell you what, though, we'll get a whole slew of rocks and belt them some good ones." We started down the steps. "Remember the story in the Bible about David. He killed a giant with a rock, and he was just a kid."

"He had a slingshot, didn't he?"

"Yes," I said, "but we don't need one." I moved my arm in a warm-up motion. "We got good Oklahoma arms that sure have throwed a lot of rocks."

It seemed strange gathering up rocks in the moonlight. I remembered how Hansel and Gretel had done that in the story to mark their way home. We weren't going anywhere, but I felt just like we were getting ready to fight a wicked witch. Somehow there under the light of the moon that night I knew something important and dangerous was about to happen.

Guilt was starting to rise up and make me feel sort of choked. H.J. had been asleep. I should of left him that way. "Ain't you tired?" I asked when the rock pile was big beside our nest in the weeds. "You can go on in if you want to."

"Shoot, no." He shook his head. "This is fun."

Of course I knew he wouldn't go, but I felt better because I had asked. We settled down to wait. Maybe I'd been wrong about danger. The night was quiet, just the gentle sound of tree frogs came to our ears. H.J. leaned against me and closed his eyes. No matter, I could wake him up if the coyotes did come. If they didn't we'd go back inside come daylight and climb into our own beds. He'd be disappointed, though, because he was looking forward to throwing his rocks, fighting like David. For a while scratching at chigger bites kept me awake, but then my eyes started growing awful heavy. Maybe I'd just lean over in the grass and rest a little. Don't go to sleep, I told myself. Well, what if I did for just a minute? Hadn't I heard them last night, me even in the house?

They didn't yelp. At least I don't think it was a sound that woke me up. It was more of a feeling, that same feeling of fear that I'd had earlier. Without disturbing H.J., I pulled myself up real slow. They were there in back of the chicken house, two coyotes, down on their bellies and working their way toward the broken-down part of the wall.

There might be another one, already inside sneaking up on one of Mama's hens. "H.J." I shook him and pointed. "Be real still. I'm going around to the other side, through the door. When I yell, you start throwing rocks at them two real hard. Coyotes won't hurt you," I reminded him. "They're scareder of you than you are of them."

He nodded and reached for rocks.

I was gone then, through the weeds and around the edge of the henhouse. My hands were full of big rocks. If there was a coyote crawling in the hole, he'd be surprised by what met him.

It was me that was surprised, though. Surprised and terrified by the scream that ripped through the still night. H.J. It was H.J., and something was wrong. Something was very very wrong.

My grip tightened on the rocks in my hand, and my feet moved fast, faster than I'd ever thought they could. Still, that short distance seemed so far, back around the chicken house corner. It seemed to take so long to reach my little brother.

He was there flattened against the wall, not far from the broken-down part. In front of him was a dog, snarling and threatening. Ring, I thought at first, but then I saw that it wasn't. The dog was brown and white instead of black, and it was big, even bigger than Ring.

I had to think quick. If I threw the rocks, likely the dog would go for H.J. He didn't show no sign of being the type to run.

"Don't move." I sort of breathed the words to H.J. "Don't move at all till I tell you."

"I made the coyotes run," he said, and he was crying.

"Shush. Don't talk now and don't move till I say so. Then you run, run for Papa." Even there like that, with my heart pounding, I realized I'd said the wrong thing. Run for Mama I should of said, because Papa wouldn't come, but I didn't waste words correcting myself. H.J. would get the only help there was. It wouldn't do me any good, though, Mama couldn't get there in time to help me.

I took one step real easy and slow toward the chicken house wall, then another, and my back was up against it like H.J.'s. The dog looked at me and snarled. In the moonlight I could see its terrible teeth.

"Watch me," I whispered. "Every time I slide over a step, you do the same thing. Keep a good distance between us. When I say run, go, but not before. I got to get his attention."

I took another sliding step, so did H.J. The dog looked my way, but his angry growl turned back to H.J. If either one of us made any real movements now, it would be H.J. torn by those great teeth. "Easy." I moved my foot very slowly. "You're being real brave, just like David."

"I got a rock. You want me to heave it at him?"

"No. No. Just don't do anything but move real slow till I say. Then run. You run, hear me." He was crying, but I was pretty sure he'd do what I said.

Timidy, ain't she? The old taunt went through my mind. No, no, she ain't timidy, I answered. She got her little brother into this, and she will get him out. I inched down another step, so did H.J.

There was a pretty good space between me and H.J. The dog looked from one of us to the other, growling, snapping, trying to decide which of us to go for first. I felt the rocks in my hand. If I threw now, I was pretty sure it would be me that got attacked and that H.J. could get away.

"Run, run now." I threw the rock hard, praying it might strike the dog's head, but I didn't see because I closed my eyes and threw again. The snarling was fierce, but nothing touched me.

With my arm shielding my face, I opened my eyes. There were two forms before me, two dogs, and they were fighting each other, growling and rolling in a death lock.

"Ring!" Even with his body so mixed with the other one, I knew. It was Ring, and he was fighting for me. I didn't even think to move. My eyes were fastened on the fight.

"Jessie!" The scream jerked me back. It was Papa's voice! It was Papa running toward me with his gun. "Jessie, run, girl! Out of the way of my shot!"

I moved then, and I yelled too. "No! Oh, no, Papa, don't shoot now. You'd hit Ring. Ring come for me, Papa." I was beside him then. I saw the dogs rear, and I heard Papa's shot.

I closed my eyes and buried my face in my hands. Papa shot again, and I had to look. Both dogs was on the ground, but then one got up. Ring got up, and he whimpered, like a baby crying.

Papa's arm was on my shoulder. "He's OK. Stand still, don't scare him, and he'll come to you." I felt like my heart would break with the wonderful joy of it. Me standing there in the summer moonlight, Papa's hand on my shoulder, and Ring coming to me, slow and shy, but coming to me.

H.J. and Mama were back there behind us. "You going to have to shoot Ring, Papa?" H.J. said it real quiet.

Papa answered real quiet too, but we all heard him. "No, oh, no," he said. "Ring is a blessed gift."